# LOVABYE DRAGON

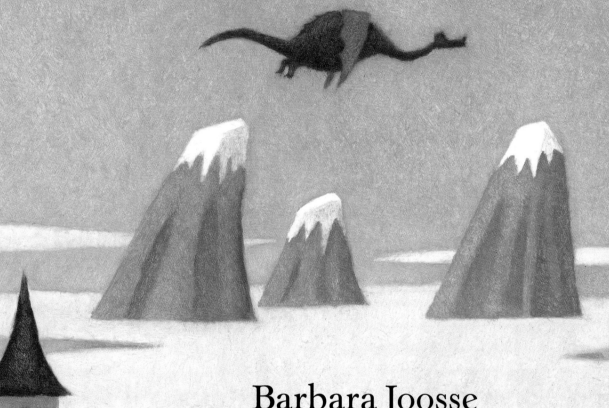

Barbara Joosse

illustrated *by* Randy Cecil

WALKER BOOKS
AND SUBSIDIARIES
LONDON · BOSTON · SYDNEY · AUCKLAND

*O*nce there was a girl

an all-alone girl

in her own little bed

in her own little room

in her own little castle

who didn't have

a dragon

for a friend.

And there was a dragon

   an all-alone dragon

in his big dragon nest

in his big dragon cave

in his big dragon mountain

who dreamed

   of a girl

      for a friend.

Oh, she cried silver tears

    many, many tears

so wishing for a dragon

so *lonely* for a dragon

and they trickled down the stairs

past a teeny-tiny mouse in his teeny-tiny house

past a boat in the moat

past a frog in the bog

round a bend in the glen

to the mountain with the cave

and the dragon.

Snore-asleep was the dragon

dream-asleep was the dragon

but the trickle of tears

   little *tickle* of tears

woke him up.

**Gluk!**

Dragon followed the trail

the little silver trail

round the bend in the glen

past the frog in the bog

past the boat in the moat

past the teeny-tiny mouse

in his teeny-tiny house ...

to the castle and the room and the girl.

Came a rumble and tumble
that might've been a giant but it wasn't
and might've been a monster but it wasn't
and might've been a dragon …

# AND IT WAS!

"I am here!" roared Dragon.

"You're a dear!" whispered Girl.

"I found you!" roared Dragon.

"As I wished," whispered Girl.

Now they'd found each other
and found *out* about each other
and they marched and they sang
all the live-long day

and they slid and they hid

till the deep, dark night.

All right.

On the outside, Girl is little.

On the outside, Dragon's biggle.

But they're *just* the same size

   *exactly* the same size

in the middle.

Dragon makes a fire

such a roasty, toasty fire

and he roars a dragon roar

such a rum-below *roar*

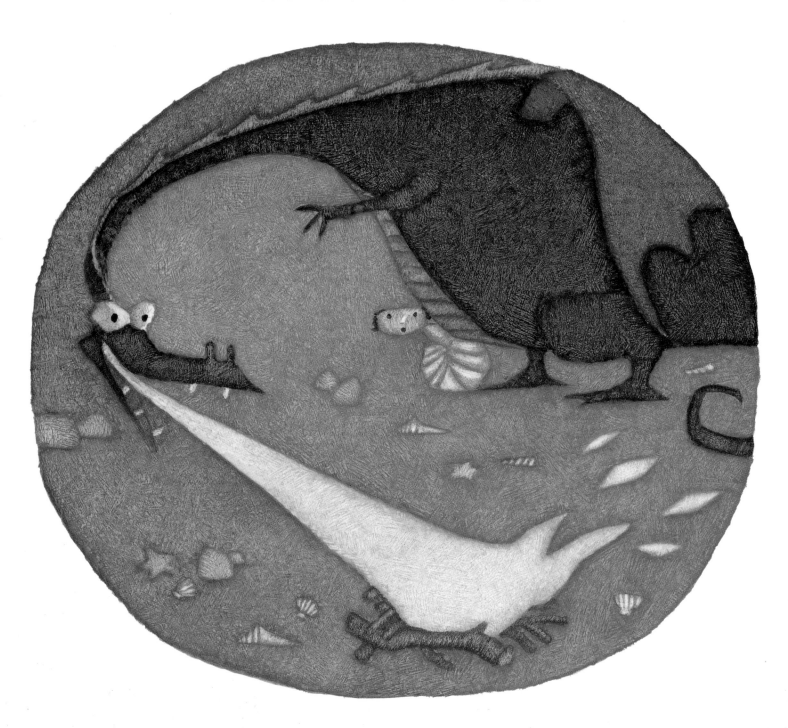

that the giants and the monsters never growl nevermore

and she's lonely for a dragon nevermore.

Now she sings little songs

little lovabye songs

and he wraps his tail around her

so gently, all around her.

Now they're friends.

Best friends.

For ever friends.

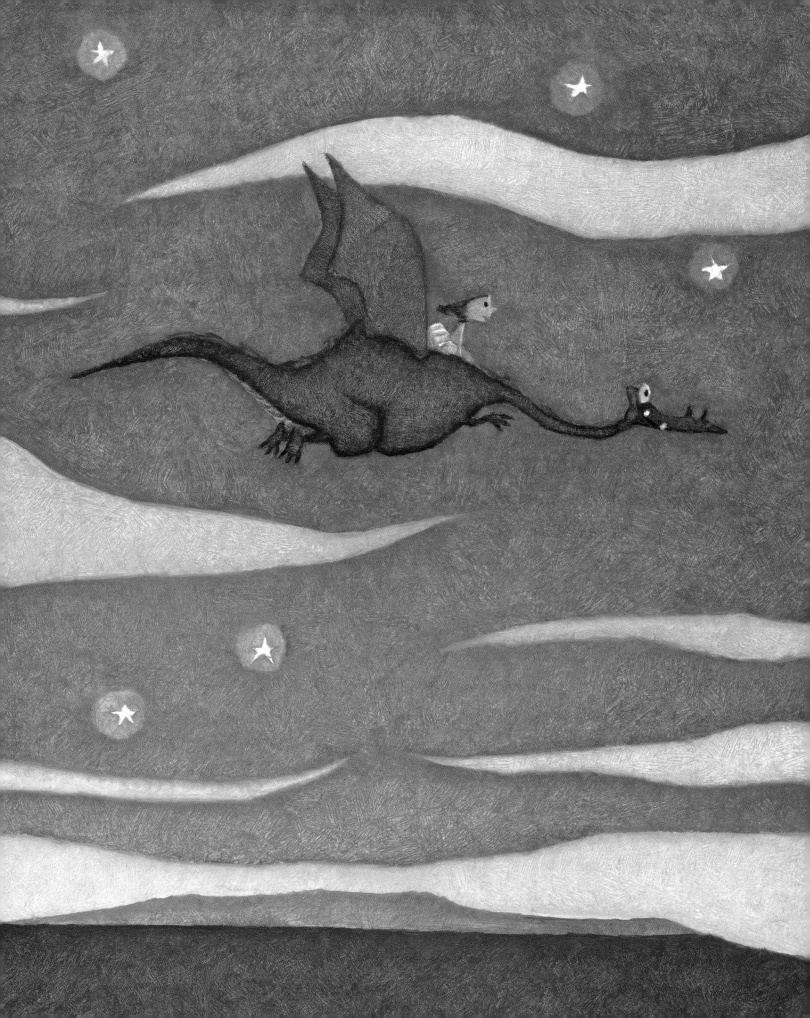

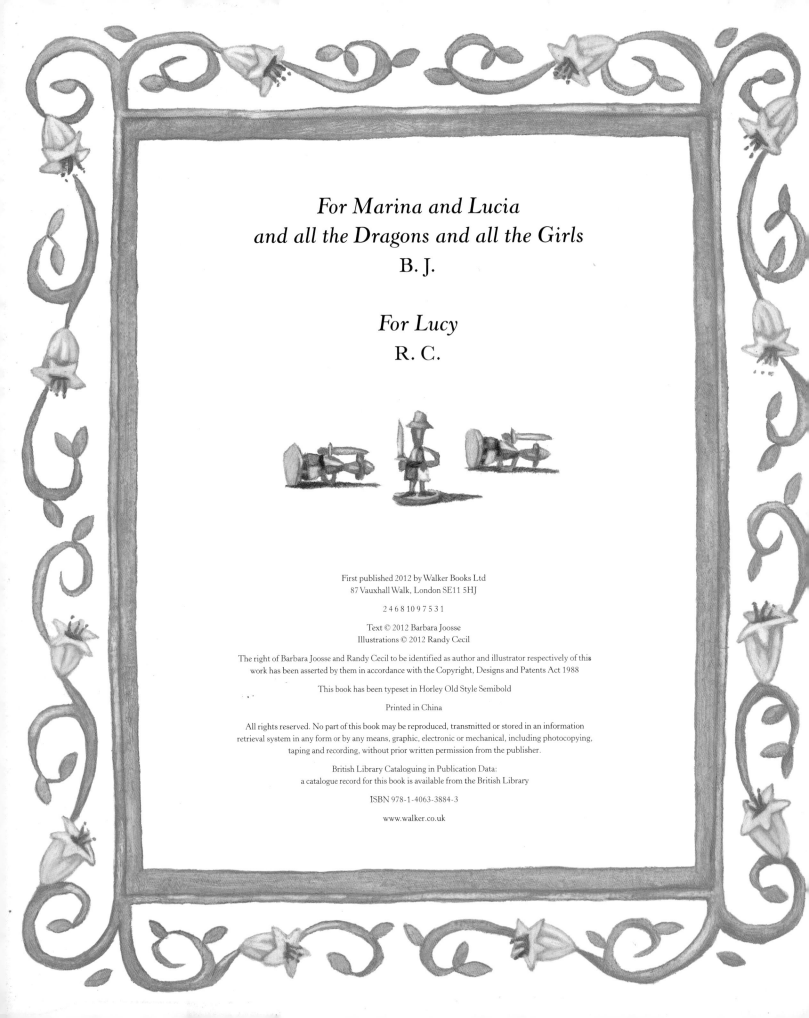

*For Marina and Lucia
and all the Dragons and all the Girls*
B. J.

*For Lucy*
R. C.

First published 2012 by Walker Books Ltd
87 Vauxhall Walk, London SE11 5HJ

2 4 6 8 10 9 7 5 3 1

Text © 2012 Barbara Joosse
Illustrations © 2012 Randy Cecil

The right of Barbara Joosse and Randy Cecil to be identified as author and illustrator respectively of this
work has been asserted by them in accordance with the Copyright, Designs and Patents Act 1988

This book has been typeset in Horley Old Style Semibold

Printed in China

British Library Cataloguing in Publication Data:
a catalogue record for this book is available from the British Library

ISBN 978-1-4063-3884-3

www.walker.co.uk